ANIMAL
CRACKERS

A BIRTHDAY FOR BLUEBELL

★ ROSE IMPEY ★ SHOO RAYNER ★

ORCHARD BOOKS

ORCHARD BOOKS
338 Euston Road, London NW1 3BH
Orchard Books Australia
Hachette Children's Books
Level 17/207 Kent Street, Sydney NSW 2000

First published by Orchard Books in 1993
This edition published in 2008

Text © Rose Impey 1993
Illustrations © Shoo Rayner 2002

The rights of Rose Impey to be identified as the author and
Shoo Rayner to be identified as the illustrator of this Work
have been asserted by them in accordance with the
Copyright, Designs and Patents Act, 1988.

A CIP catalogue record for this book is available from the British Library.

ISBN 978 1 40830 293 4

1 3 5 7 9 10 8 6 4 2
Printed in China

Orchard Books is a division of Hachette Children's Books,
an Hachette Livre UK company.
www.hachettelivre.co.uk

A Birthday for Bluebell

Bluebell was a cow.
A very old cow.
The oldest cow in the world.
Bluebell was seventy-eight years old!

People can live to be seventy-eight.
It isn't so unusual.
But for a cow it was a record.
Bluebell was famous.
She was even on the television.

When Bluebell was seventy
she had a message from the Queen.
It said, "Well done, Bluebell".

FROM THE PALACE...

..WELL DONE,

BLUEBELL....

....THE QUEEN....

When Bluebell was seventy-one
she had a letter from the
President of America.

And a cheque for 100 dollars!

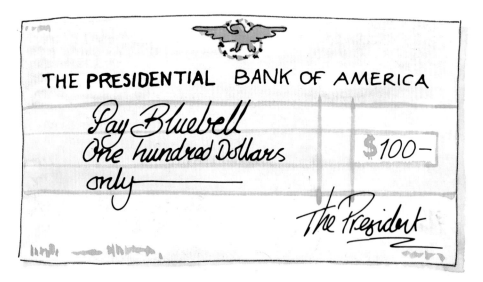

When she was seventy-two Bluebell
visited London for the first time.

She went by train.
First Class!

When she was seventy-three
Bluebell flew in Concorde.
She went to visit her grandson.
He lived in Texas.

Bluebell went for a trip
in a hot air balloon
when she was seventy-four.
It was slower than Concorde,
but she liked it.

When she was seventy-five
Bluebell did a parachute jump.
She had her picture in the paper.

But her friends began to worry
that she might break her leg
or end up in hospital.
"After all," they said,
"she *is* seventy-five years old."

When she was seventy-six
her friends told Bluebell,

Bluebell was surprised.
She didn't feel old.

When Bluebell was seventy-seven
her friends gave her a television.
Then Bluebell slowed down.

She watched television all day,
every day of the week.
She never did anything else.
Her friends were sorry
they had ever given her a television.

"There is nothing else
I want now," said Bluebell.
"Nothing in the world."

So when Bluebell was seventy-eight
her friends couldn't decide
what to get her.

What can you get for a cow
who has everything?

A cow who has been everywhere.

"There must be something,"
they thought.
So they each tried to find out
what Bluebell would like.

Goat showed her his holiday photos.
Ski-ing in Spain.

"Do you like holidays?" he asked.
But Bluebell shook her head.

I am happy to stay at home, now I am old.

Donkey showed Bluebell his new
CD player.

"Would you like one?" he said.
But Bluebell shook her head.

Pig showed Bluebell tickets
for the new Adventure Fun Park.

"Would you like to go?" she said.
But Bluebell shook her head.
"It would only make me dizzy,"
she said. "I am too old for fun parks."

"Bluebell is so boring,"
said Hen.

"She used to be such good fun,"
said Pig.

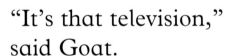

"It's our fault,"
said Donkey.

"It's that television,"
said Goat.

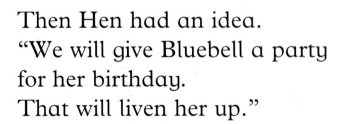

Then Hen had an idea.
"We will give Bluebell a party
for her birthday.
That will liven her up."

"A party is a good idea,"
said Goat. "But Bluebell
has had parties before."
"Not a fancy dress party,"
said Hen.
"With party games," said Pig.
"And party music," said Donkey.
"And no television!" said Goat.

For the next week
the animals were busy
making their plans.
They didn't tell Bluebell.
They wanted it to be a surprise.

Every day Bluebell watched television,
as usual.
No one came round to visit.
No one asked her to go out
for a walk
or a swim.
Bluebell began to feel lonely.

"A television is nice," she said,
"but not as nice as friends."

Bluebell went out
to look for her friends.
But her friends were too busy.

"Sorry, Bluebell, just going out,"
said Goat.

"No time to stop," said Pig.

"Too much to do," said Donkey.

"See you later," said Hen.

Bluebell went home
feeling very sorry for herself.
"Nobody wants me any more,"
she said. "Now I am old."

On Saturday morning
Bluebell got out of bed.
She didn't turn on her television.
She just sat in her chair
feeling miserable.

But then the postman came.
He brought her lots of cards.
They made her smile.

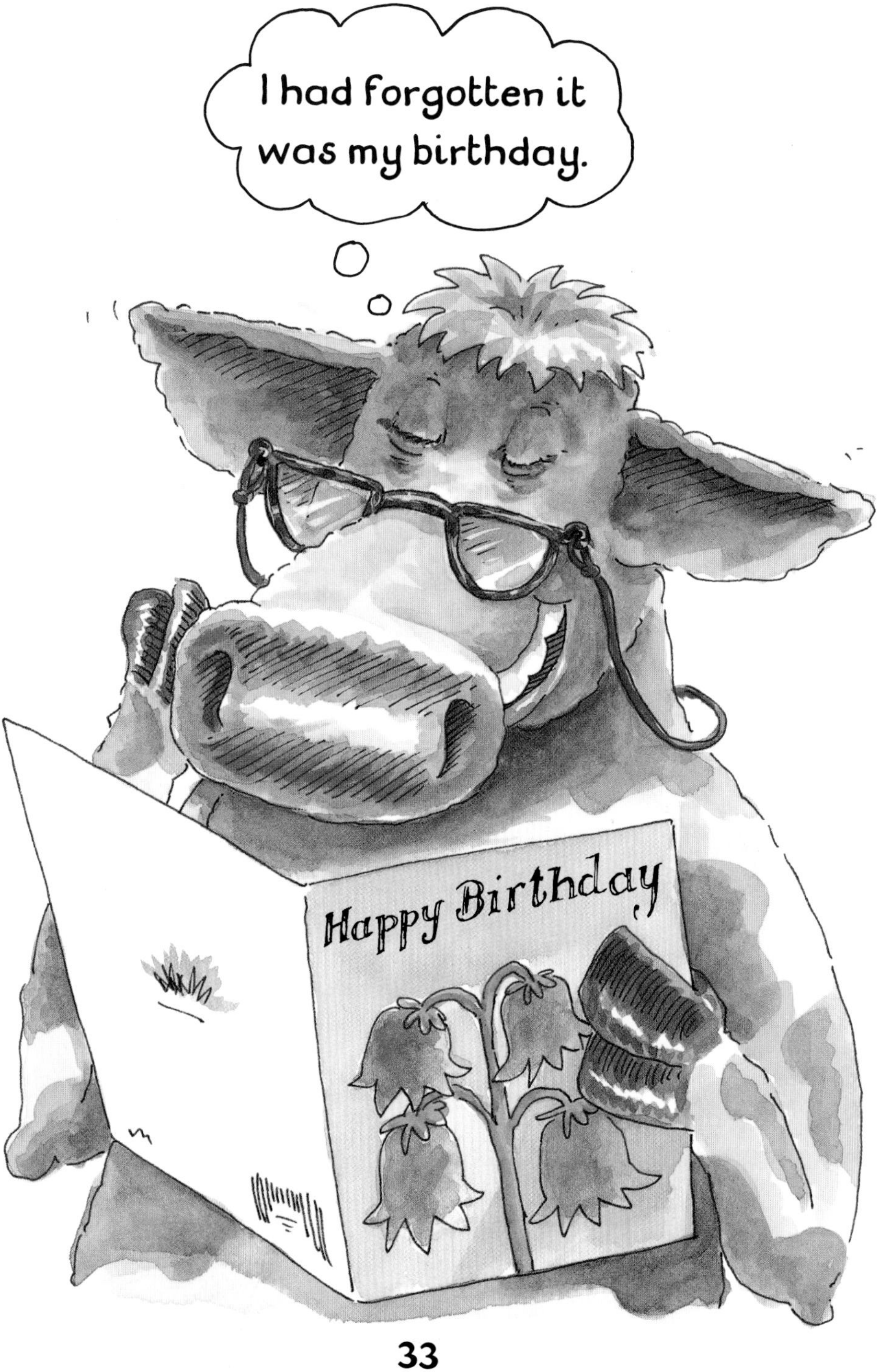
I had forgotten it was my birthday.
Happy Birthday

Hen knocked at the door.
She was holding a large box.
"Happy birthday, Bluebell,"
she said.
"You look funny," said Bluebell.
"What is in that box?"
"Open it and see," said Hen.

COSTUME
HIRE Co.

It was a fancy dress outfit.
"I can't wear that," said Bluebell.
"I am too old to dress up."
"Nonsense," said Hen.
"You are as old as you feel.
Come on, put it on.
Everyone will be here soon."

When the other animals arrived
Bluebell was dressed
and ready for the party.
"Happy birthday, Bluebell,"
said Donkey
and Pig
and Goat.

Bluebell couldn't stop laughing.
"You all look silly," she said.
"So do you," said Hen.
"Who cares," said Goat.
"Time for the games," said Pig.

First they played
Pin the tail on the donkey.
"Be careful," said Donkey.

Then they played
Apple Bobbing

and Musical Bumps

and Pass the Parcel.

The other animals let Bluebell win.
After all, it was her birthday.

Next Donkey put on some music and all the animals danced. Everyone danced with Bluebell because it was her birthday.

And then they had the party food.
Hen had cooked it all.
She had made a cake too.

There were seventy-eight candles.
Bluebell tried to blow them out.
She was soon out of breath.
The other animals had to help her.

"You are not as fit
as you were," said Hen.
"Too much television," said Goat.
"Tomorrow we will go for a walk,"
said Pig.
"And a swim," said Donkey.

"Yes," said Hen.
"We have to get you fit
if you are going to live
to be a hundred."

"Well," said Bluebell,
"next year I think I might try
wind-surfing. I have always
wanted to try wind-surfing."
"Why not," said the other
animals. "After all,
you *are* only seventy-eight."

Hello dears!

Crack-A-Joke

What do cows play at parties?
Moosical chairs!

What do you get if you cross a cow
and a sheep and a goat?
The Milky Baa Kid!

What do you get if
you cross a cow
with a bird?
Cheep milk!

Who steals cattle?
A beef burglar!

What do you get if you a cross a cow with a duck?
Cream quackers!

What do you call an Arctic cow?
An eskimoo!

ANIMAL
CRACKERS

COLLECT ALL THE
ANIMAL CRACKERS BOOKS!

A Birthday for Bluebell	978 1 40830 293 4	£4.99
Too Many Babies	978 1 40830 294 1	£4.99
Hot Dog Harris	978 1 40830 295 8	£4.99
Sleepy Sammy	978 1 40830 296 5	£4.99
Precious Potter	978 1 40830 297 2	£4.99
Phew Sidney	978 1 40830 298 9	£4.99
Open Wide Wilbur	978 1 40830 299 6	£4.99
We Want William	978 1 40830 300 9	£4.99

All priced at £4.99

Orchard Colour Crunchies are available from all good bookshops, or can be
ordered direct from the publisher:
Orchard Books, PO BOX 29, Douglas IM99 1BQ
Credit card orders please telephone 01624 836000
or fax 01624 837033 or visit our internet site: www.orchardbooks.co.uk
or e-mail: bookshop@enterprise.net for details.
To order please quote title, author and ISBN
and your full name and address.
Cheques and postal orders should be made payable to 'Bookpost plc.'
Postage and packing is FREE within the UK
(overseas customers should add £2.00 per book).
Prices and availability are subject to change.